MagNifiCent TaleS ™

Daniel for Lunch

The Tasty Tale of Daniel in the Lions' Den

Based on Daniel 6

Kelly Pulley

David C Cook

transforming lives together

DANIEL FOR LUNCH
Published by David C Cook
4050 Lee Vance View
Colorado Springs, CO 80918 U.S.A.

David C Cook Distribution Canada
55 Woodslee Avenue, Paris, Ontario, Canada N3L 3E5

David C Cook U.K., Kingsway Communications
Eastbourne, East Sussex BN23 6NT, England

The graphic circle C logo is a registered trademark of David C Cook.

LCCN 2012945763
ISBN 978-1-4347-0367-5
eISBN 978-1-4347-0588-4

Art and Text © 2012 Kelly Pulley

The Team: Susan Tjaden, Amy Konyndyk, Jack Campbell, Karen Athen

Manufactured in Hong Kong in October 2012 by Printplus Limited.
First Edition 2012

1 2 3 4 5 6 7 8 9 10

090512

This book is dedicated to those
special friends and mentors who were
placed in my path to inspire and
encourage me during this journey
from illustrator to author.
And to God, who humbles me with
His Magnificent stories.

The work of a king can be hard and demanding,
so King Darius wanted some help with commanding.
He gathered some helpers to lend him a hand.
They cared for his stuff. They protected his land.

A worker named Daniel was clearly the best,
so the king made him boss over all of the rest.
But the rest were not happy with Daniel, their boss.
The king, they agreed, should give Daniel the toss!

They said, "Daniel must go,
then the choice will be clear
whom the king should make boss
from the helpers still here!"

They watched Daniel to see if he did something bad.
They would run and they'd tattle on him if he had.
They watched night. They watched day.
But they never did find
even one little thing
that would change the king's mind.

They whined, "Daniel is faithful,
he's good, and he's wise.
He *always* works hard
and he *never* tells lies.
If there's one little thing we might use, then it's this:
He prays every day. Not a day does he miss."
"That's it!" said a helper.
"We've got him! He's through!
We'll make praying a crime!
Yes, that's *just* what we'll do!
We'll bamboozle the king into making it wrong,
then Daniel, our boss, won't be boss for too long!"

So they ran to the king, feeling ever so clever.
They greeted the king saying, "King, live forever!
All we helpers agree that a law should be made
that says people who pray any prayers
that are prayed,
must pray them to *you* because *you* are the best!

They must *not* pray to men or
to gods or the rest!
If they dare say a prayer to some other
than you, then they'll sleep with the
lions! Have lunch with
them too!"

King Darius liked how the law made him feel.
So he wrote it all down and he gave it his seal.
Now the law had been signed. It could not be undone.
The helpers all grinned. Surely Daniel was done.
The law was proclaimed. One and all understood.
They must pray to the king. Hungry lions weren't good!

Now when Daniel got home, he did just as before.
He went straight to his window
and knelt on the floor.

He prayed only to God. Daniel broke the king's law,
as the helpers who spied while he prayed clearly saw.

Now they questioned the king,
feeling ever so clever,
"Can the law be undone?"
And the king answered, "Never!"
They said, "Daniel still prays to his God every day!
He cares nothing for you or the things that you say!
He must sleep with the lions! The law is quite clear!
You signed it yourself! See, your seal is right here!"

So the king gave the order to some of his men,
that Daniel be thrown in the lions' dark den.
He was brought to the pit. Then they pitched him inside.
King Darius poked in his head as he cried,
"May your God whom you serve without cease every day
rescue you from the lions and keep you okay!"

Now, the king was quite worried because of his hunch
that the lions were hungry and Daniel was lunch!
Too worried to sleep and too worried to eat,
when the sun began rising, he jumped to his feet.

He ran lickety-split to the den from his room.
He was worried that Daniel had met with his doom.

"Did your God whom you serve keep you safe?"
the king cried.

"Yes, an angel from God saved me!" Daniel replied.
"He calmed all the lions so none would attack
and munch me for lunch or perhaps for a snack."

The king was delighted that Daniel was free!
To his kingdom the king then declared by decree,
"Whenever you pray any prayers that you pray,
no matter the place or the time of the day,
don't pray them to men! And don't pray them to me!
Just pray them to God, who let Daniel go free!
He calmed all the lions. He stopped their attack.
They didn't munch Daniel for lunch or a snack!"

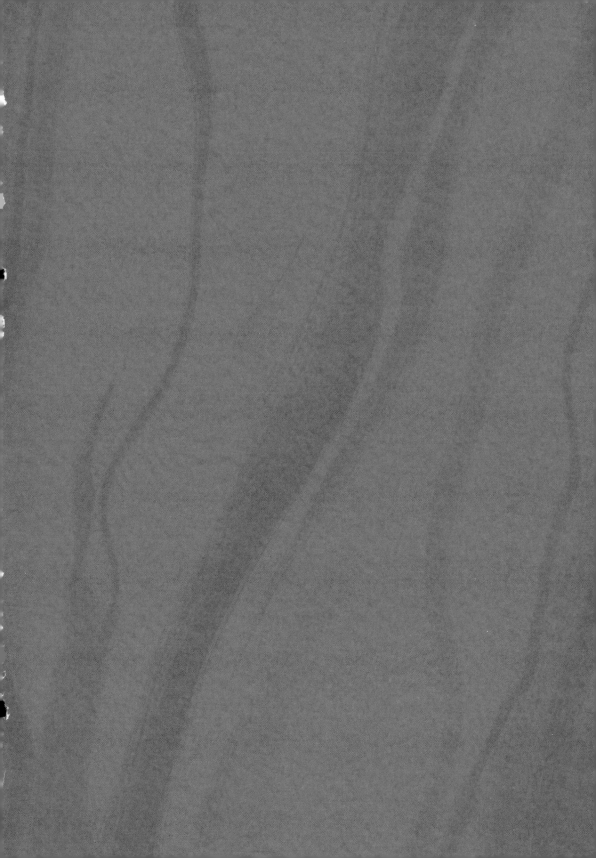